It's Mine!

DRAGONFLY BOOKS PUBLISHED BY ALFRED A. KNOPF, INC.

Copyright © 1985, 1986 by Leo Lionni

Manufactured in the United States of America

Library of Congress Cataloging-in-Publication Data
Lionni, Leo. It's mine!
Summary: Three selfish frogs quarrel over who owns their pond and
island, until a storm makes them value the benefits of sharing.
1. Children's stories, American. [1. Selfishness—Fiction.
2. Sharing—Fiction. 3. Frogs—Fiction.]
I. Title. II. Title: It's Mine! PZ7.L6634It   1986 [E] 85-190
ISBN: 0-394-87000-X (trade)
        0-394-97000-4 (library binding)
        0-679-88084-4 (paperback)
First Dragonfly Books edition: March 1996

10 9 8 7 6 5 4 3 2

It's Mine!

by Leo Lionni

Dragonfly Books
Alfred A. Knopf • New York

In the middle of Rainbow Pond
there was a small island.
Smooth pebbles lined its beaches,
and it was covered with ferns
and leafy weeds.

On the island lived three quarrelsome frogs
named Milton, Rupert, and Lydia. They quarreled
and quibbled from dawn to dusk.

"Stay out of the pond!" yelled Milton. "The water is mine."

"Get off the island!" shouted Rupert. "The earth is mine."

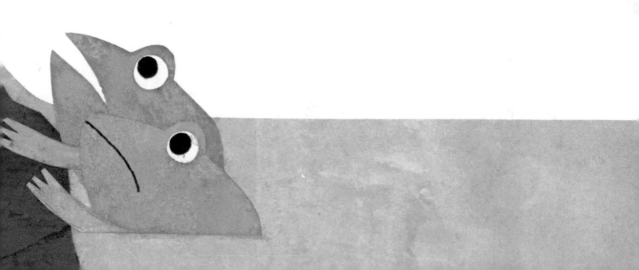

"The air is mine!" screamed Lydia as she leaped
to catch a butterfly. And so it went.

One day a large toad appeared before them.

"I live on the other side of the island," he said, "but I can hear you shouting 'It's mine! It's mine! It's mine!' all day long. There is no peace because of your endless bickering. You can't go on like this!" With that the toad slowly turned around and hopped away through the weeds.

No sooner had he left than Milton ran off with a large
worm. The others hopped after him. "Worms are
for everybody!" they cried.

But Milton croaked defiantly, "Not this one. It's mine!"

Suddenly the sky darkened and a rumble
of distant thunder circled the island.
Rain filled the air, and the water turned to
mud. The island grew smaller and smaller
as it was swallowed up by the rising
flood. The frogs were scared.

Desperately they clung to the few slippery stones that still rose above the wild, dark water. But soon these too began to disappear.

There was only one rock left and there the frogs huddled, trembling from cold and fright. But they felt better now that they were together, sharing the same fears and hopes. Little by little the flood subsided. The rain fell gently and then stopped altogether.

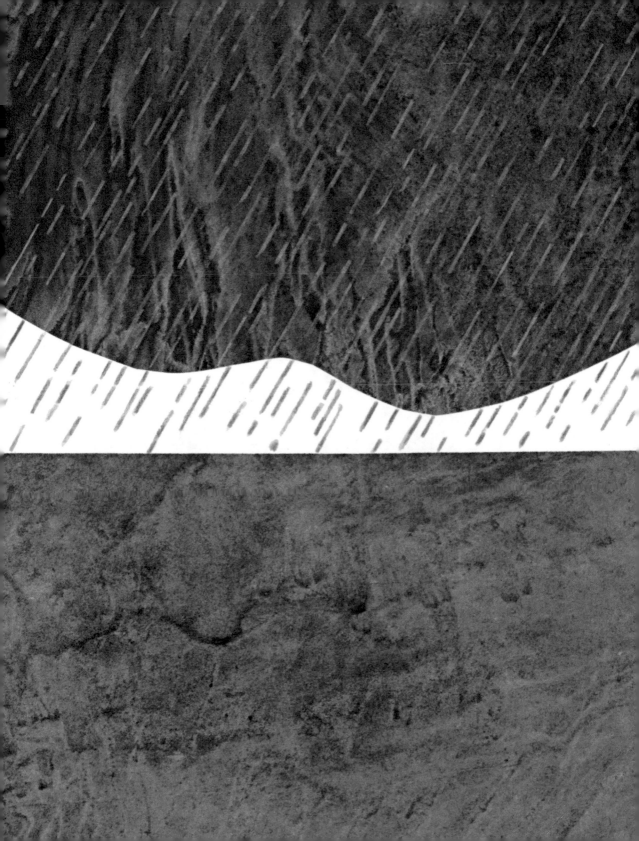

But look! The large rock that had saved them was no rock at all.
"You saved us!" shouted the frogs when they recognized the toad.

The next morning the water had cleared. Sunrays
chased silver minnows on the sandy bottom of the pond.
Joyfully the frogs jumped in, and side by side
they swam all around the island.

Together they leaped after the swarms of
butterflies that filled the air.

And later, when they rested in the weeds, they felt happy
in a way they had never been before.

"Isn't it peaceful," said Milton.
"And isn't it beautiful," said Rupert.
"And do you know what else?" said Lydia.
"No, what?" the others asked.
"It's ours!" she said.

Leo Lionni was born in Holland and as a child taught himself to draw by copying the work of the masters in Amsterdam's museums. He received a Ph.D. in economics from the University of Genoa and came to this country in 1939 with his wife, Nora, and two young sons. He has been involved in the world of graphic arts ever since. Internationally recognized as an artist, designer, sculptor, and author of children's books, he is the recipient of the 1984 American Institute of Graphic Arts Gold Medal and is a four-time Caldecott Honor Book winner for *Inch by Inch, Frederick, Swimmy,* and *Alexander and the Wind-Up Mouse.*

The Lionnis divide their time between a New York apartment and a seventeenth-century farmhouse in Tuscany, Italy.